Someday

by Diane Paterson

BRADBURY PRESS   NEW YORK

Maxwell Macmillan Canada   Toronto
Maxwell Macmillan International
New York   Oxford   Singapore   Sydney

For Captain James J. Gully

Bradbury Press
Macmillan Publishing Company
866 Third Avenue
New York, NY 10022

Maxwell Macmillan Canada, Inc.
1200 Eglinton Avenue East
Suite 200
Don Mills, Ontario M3C 3N1

Macmillan Publishing Company is part of the Maxwell
Communication Group of Companies.

First American edition
Printed and bound in Hong Kong by
South China Printing Company (1988) Ltd.

10 9 8 7 6 5 4 3 2 1
The text of this book is set in ITC Clearface.
The illustrations are rendered in watercolor.

LIBRARY OF CONGRESS CATALOGING-IN-PUBLICATION DATA
Paterson, Diane, date.
Someday / by Diane Paterson.
p.   cm.
Summary: Animal friends go for a sail on the boat "Someday."
ISBN 0-02-770565-X
[1. Boats and boating—Fiction. 2. Sailing—Fiction.
3. Animals—Fiction.] I. Title.
PZ7.P2727Sr   1993
[E]—dc20   92-11401

Contents

Just Right

A sea gull went to the beach. He tossed pebbles into the water. He rolled up his pants and waded.

"I like the beach," said Gull.

Then he saw a boat. It was bouncing over the waves.

"Someday I will have a boat," Gull said. "Friday, Saturday . . . today *is* someday! I will find a boat now."

He went to the boatyard.

He looked at a rowboat. It was too small. He looked at a houseboat. It was too big. Then he saw a sailboat. It was red.

"Just right," Gull said.

A crow was painting it.

"I want to buy your boat," said Gull.

"Good!" Crow said. "You can have it for only five clams."

"That is too much," said Gull.

"If you buy my boat," Crow told him, "I will also give you this cork. It is just the right size to plug a hole."

A cork like that would be good to have. It would keep water out of the boat. Gull wanted the cork, too.

"I do not have five clams," Gull said.

"That is not good," said Crow.

Gull kicked at the sand. He wanted
the sailboat with the nice big cork.
"I will find some clams," he said.
He worked hard. Soon his pockets
were filled with clams and other
things.

"Would you sell your boat for three clams and this seashell?" asked Gull. The shell was shiny and pink.

"Maybe," said Crow.

"Would you sell your boat for three clams, a seashell, and this beach pebble?"

Crow looked at the beach pebble. It was round and smooth.

"Yes!" he said. "Now you can buy my boat."

Gull jumped up and down.

Help

Gull washed and polished his new boat.

"Someday I will sail," he said, "as soon as I think of a name for my boat."

"Friday, Saturday . . . today *is* someday," he said. "I will name my boat *Someday*."

12

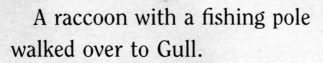

A raccoon with a fishing pole
walked over to Gull.

"What a nice boat you have," said
Raccoon.

"What a nice fishing pole you
have," said Gull.

"Take me for a ride on your boat,"
said Raccoon, "and you can use my
fishing pole."

"We can sail and fish together,"
said Gull.

Raccoon put a rubber worm on a
fishhook. He dangled it over the side.
    "Something is wrong," he said.
"The water is too far away."
    "I do not know how to put my boat
into the water," said Gull.
    "That is not good," said Raccoon.

A rabbit came by wearing swim
flippers and goggles.

"What nice goggles and flippers you
have," said Gull.

"Take me for a ride on your boat,"
said Rabbit. "We could jump off and
swim together."

"What a good idea," said Gull.

"Let's go," said Rabbit. She waited
and waited. The boat did not go.
"This is not a good boat," she said.

A pig walked by. She had a lunch bucket.

"What a wonderful boat!" she said. "It is perfect for a picnic."

Everyone was hungry. "We will take you for a ride," they said.

Pig got on.

"This is not a good boat," she said. "It does not go."

"I want to fish," said Raccoon.
"I want to swim," said Rabbit.
"I want to eat lunch," said Pig.
"I want to sail," said Gull.
"Help!" everyone hollered.

A dog heard them. He was a lifeguard.

"I'll save you!" he said.

"No, no!" everyone said. "We need help to put the boat into the water."

"I will help you get help," said Lifeguard Dog.

"Help!" he yelled.

Good Friends

Crow rushed over. "I will help," he said. Everyone cheered.

"But you will have to give me five clams," said Crow.

"We do not have five clams," Gull said.

"That is not good," said Crow.

"I have a fishing pole," said Raccoon.

"I have goggles and flippers," said Rabbit.

"I have a lunch bucket," said Pig.

"I have a whistle," said Lifeguard Dog.

"And I have good friends," said Gull.

"Good," said Crow. "I will take everything. Then I will help."

Crow told them what to do. It was
not easy. Everyone pushed and pulled.
The boat finally dropped into the
water with a splash.

Everyone got on except Crow.

"I want to go, too," he said.

"It will cost five clams," said Gull.

"I do not have five clams," said Crow. "But I have a fishing pole, goggles, flippers, and a whistle."

"Maybe you can come," said Gull.

"And I also have a bucket of lunch," said Crow.

"Welcome aboard," said Gull.

Crow got on.

And the boat did go.

"At last!" everyone said.

Lost and Found

There was plenty of wind.
It filled the sail. The boat went
faster and faster. It sailed across the
bay and out into the ocean.

"Where are we going?" asked Pig.

"Round and round and up and down," said Gull.

"We're lost!" said Crow.

"Oh no," said Pig.

The boat rocked and rolled.

"We are not lost," said Gull. "I know where we are." He pointed at Pig. "Pig is there. Raccoon, Rabbit, and Lifeguard Dog are here. And you are there, Crow."

"We are here," said Crow. "But
how do we go back?"

They sailed all day.

"Maybe we *are* lost," said Gull.

"I told you so," said Crow.

"Maybe someday we will be found," said Gull.

"I hope so," said Pig.

"Friday, Saturday . . . today *is* someday!" said Gull. "We will be found today."

Gull looked north. Rabbit and Raccoon looked south. Lifeguard Dog looked east. Crow looked west. Pig looked at the water and spilled the lunch.

"I see a ship," said Gull. "It is coming this way."

"Help!" yelled Lifeguard Dog.

The ship floated next to them.
"Help! We're lost," everyone yelled.
"I have found you," said the
captain, "so you are not lost. You
cannot be lost and found at the same
time."

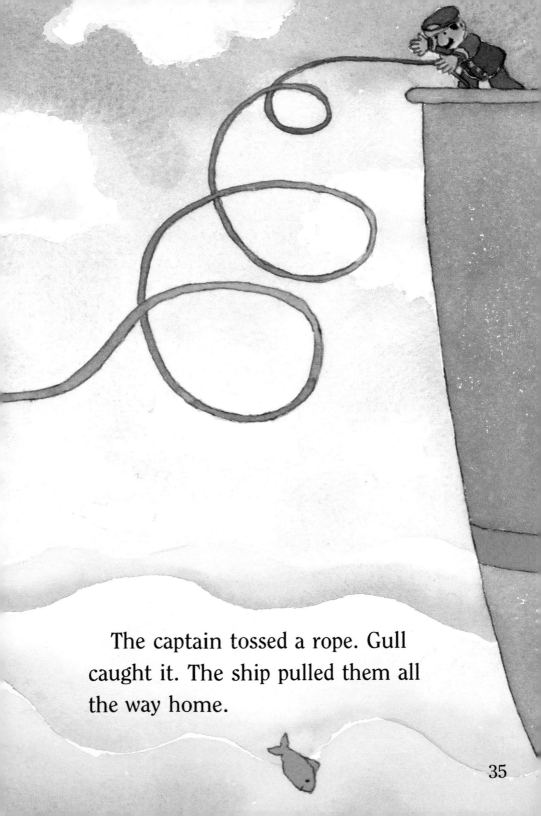

The captain tossed a rope. Gull
caught it. The ship pulled them all
the way home.

Someday

"Home at last," said Crow.

"Let's eat!" said Pig. She looked in the lunch bucket. It was empty.

"Oh no," everyone said.

"Let's go on the boat again," said Gull.

"Then we can catch a fish for dinner," said Raccoon.

"Fish! Yummy!" said Crow.

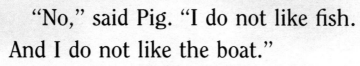

"No," said Pig. "I do not like fish. And I do not like the boat."

"Maybe someday," said Gull, "you will like fish. And maybe someday you will like the boat."

"Friday, Saturday . . . today *is* someday," said Pig. So she climbed back on the boat. Then everyone sailed away to somewhere on *Someday*. And they all had a good time. Even Pig.